moshi monsters ™

• DR. STRANGEGLOVE •

MONSTROUS BIOGRAPHIES

by Ruby Scribblez

Dr. Strangeglove
MONSTROUS BIOGRAPHIES

SUNBIRD
PENGUIN

Published by Ladybird Books Ltd 2012
A Penguin Company
Penguin Books Ltd, 80 Strand, London, WC2R 0RL, UK
Penguin Group (USA) Inc., 375 Hudson Street, New York 10014, USA
Penguin Books Australia Ltd, Camberwell Road, Camberwell,
Victoria 3124, Australia (A division of Pearson Australia Group Pty Ltd
Penguin Group (NZ), 67 Apollo Drive, Rosedale, Auckland 0632,
New Zealand (a division of Pearson New Zealand Ltd)
Canada, India, South Africa

Sunbird is a trademark of Ladybird Books Ltd

Written by Steve Cleverley and Lauren Holowaty

www.ladybird.com

ISBN: 9781409390978
001 - 10 9 8 7 6 5 4 3 2 1
Printed in China

CONTENTS

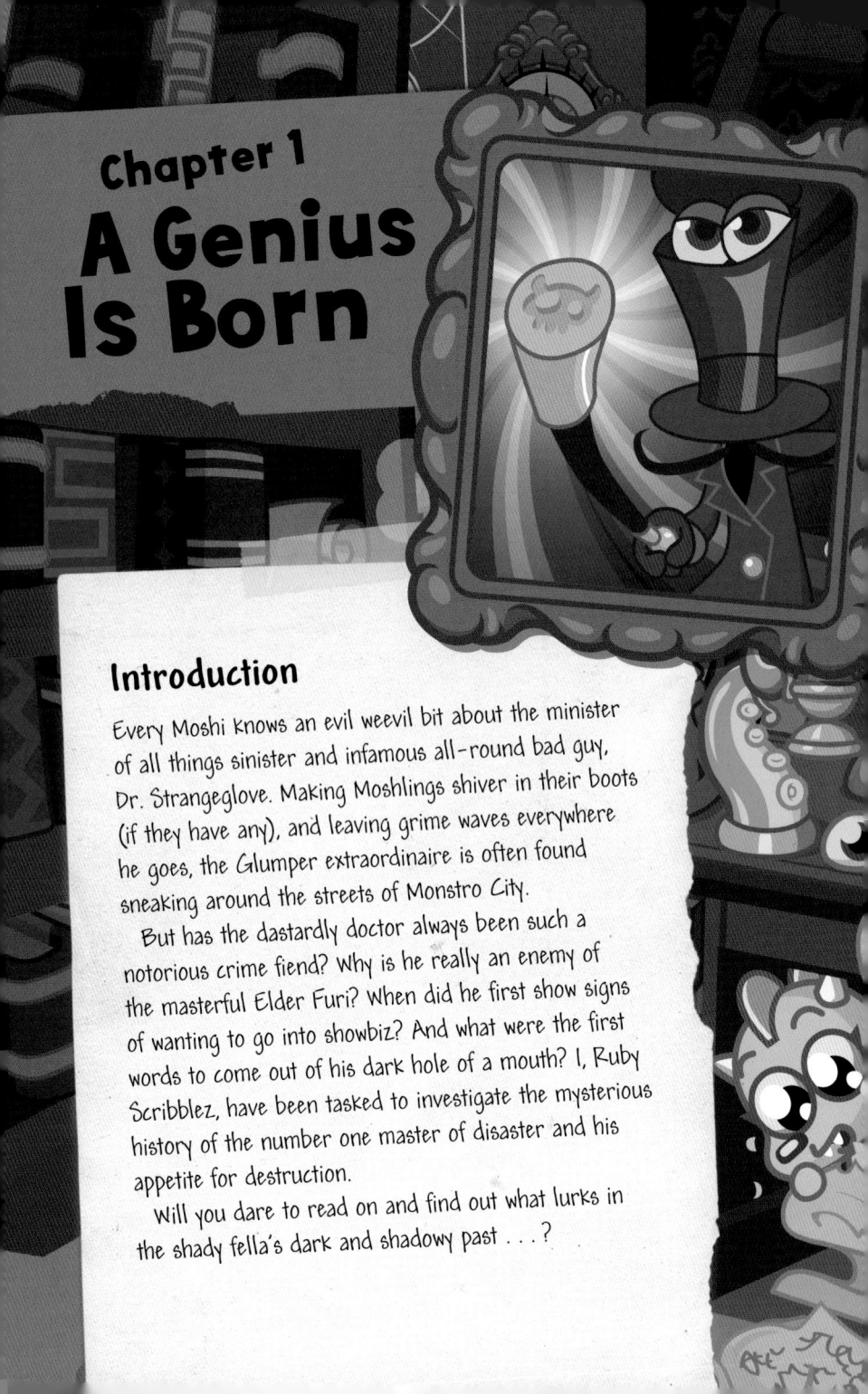

Chapter 1
A Genius Is Born

Introduction

Every Moshi knows an evil weevil bit about the minister of all things sinister and infamous all-round bad guy, Dr. Strangeglove. Making Moshlings shiver in their boots (if they have any), and leaving grime waves everywhere he goes, the Glumper extraordinaire is often found sneaking around the streets of Monstro City.

But has the dastardly doctor always been such a notorious crime fiend? Why is he really an enemy of the masterful Elder Furi? When did he first show signs of wanting to go into showbiz? And what were the first words to come out of his dark hole of a mouth? I, Ruby Scribblez, have been tasked to investigate the mysterious history of the number one master of disaster and his appetite for destruction.

Will you dare to read on and find out what lurks in the shady fella's dark and shadowy past . . . ?

From Sproggs to Troggs

When I began to explore Strangeglove's secret past, I soon found out that there is much more to this criminal mastermind than pure mischief. It seems he was born into the world an absolute genius. We don't know that much about baby Strangeglove, but we do know that he was originally named Lavender Troggs, and that for security reasons his parents have asked to remain anonymous. However, they were kind enough to give us this very sickly sweet memento of his childhood. If you scrutinize these early observations, and read in between the lines, you may be able to piece together bits of the doctor's personality, and imagine what he was like as a Moshi youngster . . .

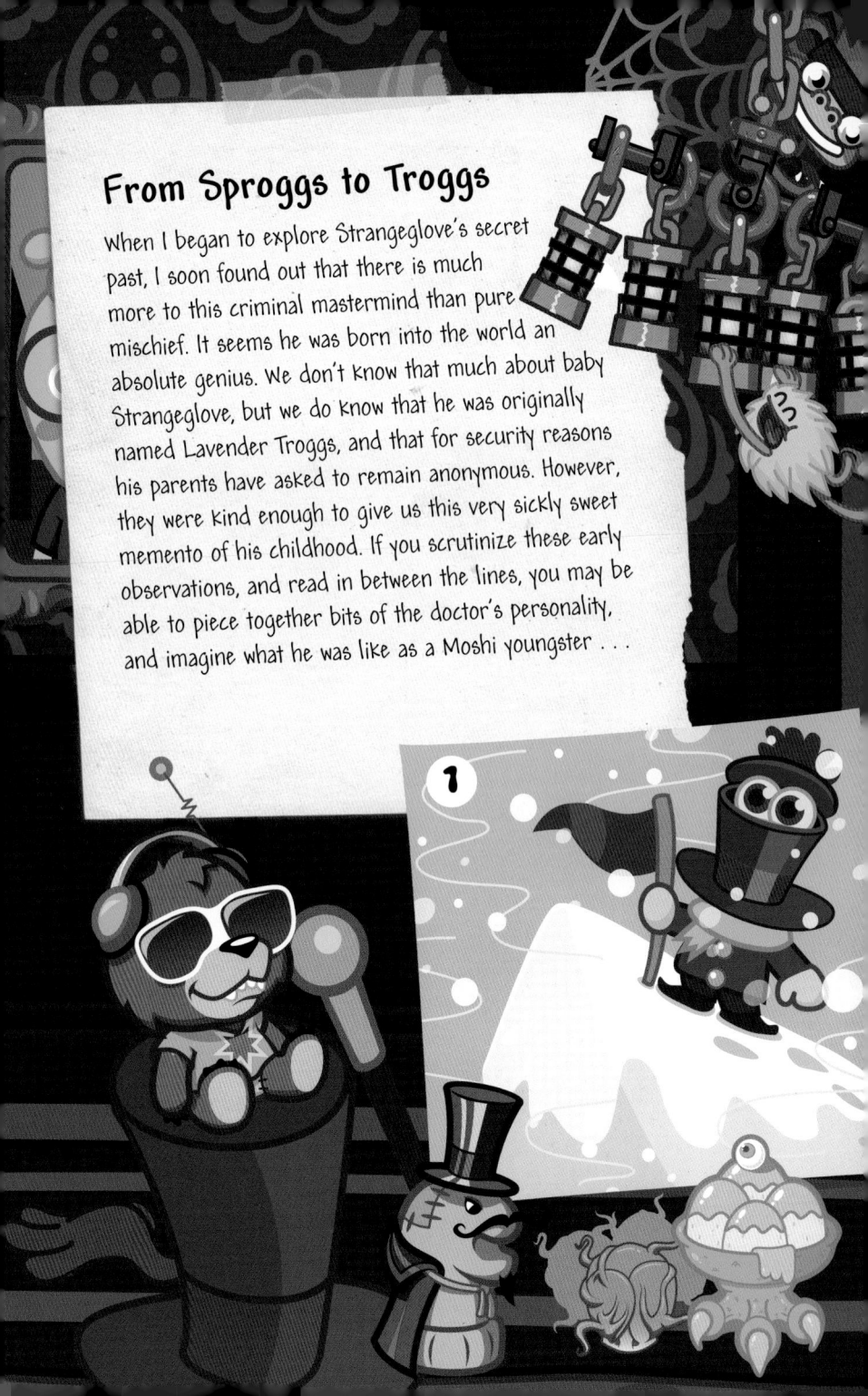

1

My First Five Years Baby Moshi Record

🖐 My First Lock of Moustache Hair:

🖐 My First Words: "Mummy, Daddy, mosheenymonodoyouthinkhesawusthingymijiggysoscious." (One of the longest words in the Moshi dictionary. His parents didn't even know what it meant!) These words were shortly followed not by a baby giggle, but a mighty "Mwaaah-haa-hah!" of course.

🖐 My First and Favourite Books: *The Complete Works of Shakesfear* and *Snore and Peas by Toadstool*

🖐 My First Toys: Baby Mastermind and Chip the Scare Bear

🖐 My Favourite Baby Foods: Mountains of Silly Sausages and Mutant Sprouts, with lashings of Eyescream Sundae piled on top

🖐 My First Clothes: The Wizard of Snoz Cloak and My First Razor-Sharp Shoes **2**

🖐 My First Toothy Peg: Note: Removed by Dr. Fang, as too vicious for a baby Moshi to have in its mouth. **3**

🖐 My First Toenails: (stuck in below) **4**

🖐 My First Steps: Conquering Mount Sillimanjaro, aged 4. The first (and only!) baby Moshi to ever do so, and not fall off. **1**

🖐 My Favourite Colour: Gold

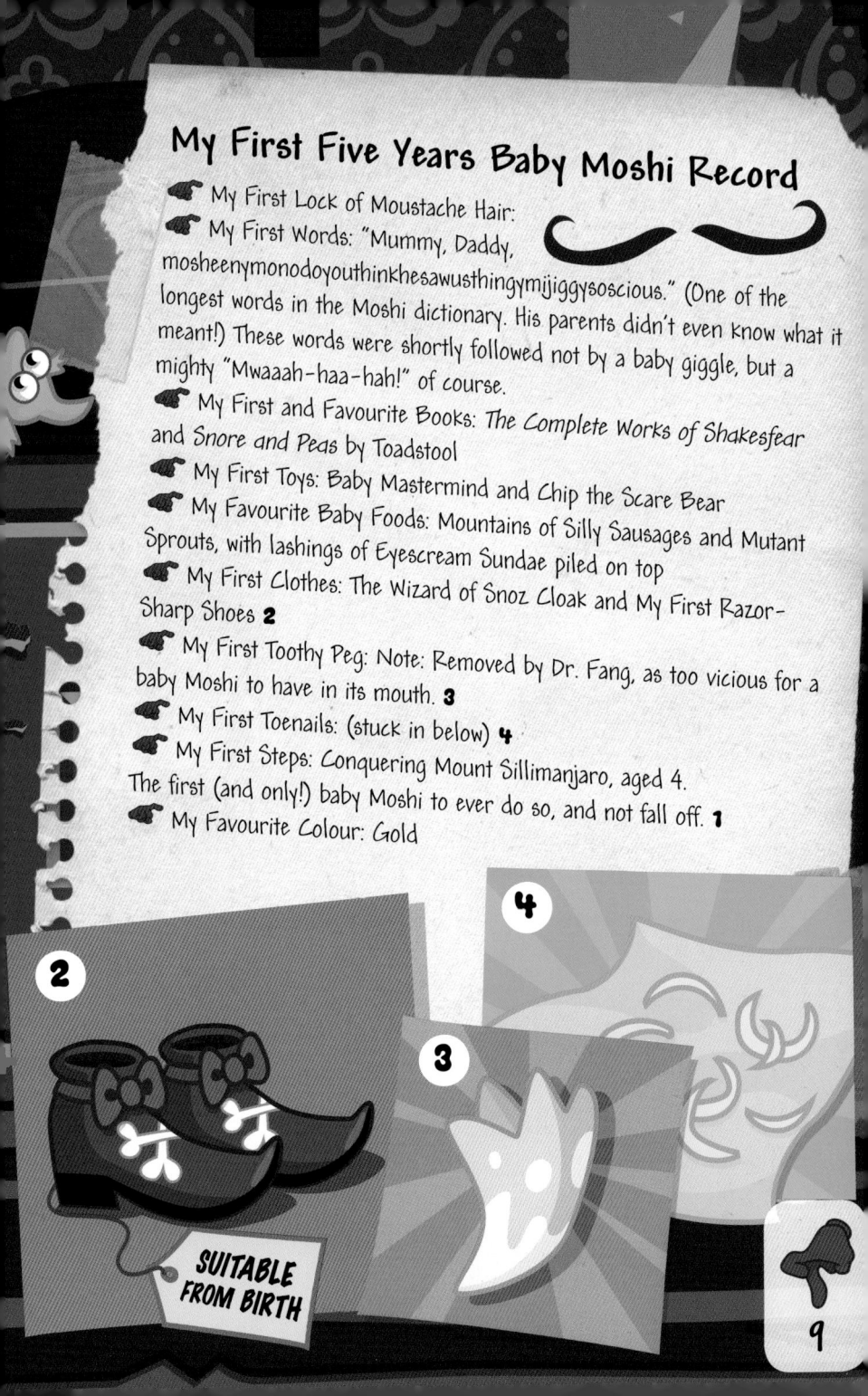

4

2

3

SUITABLE FROM BIRTH

Too Cruel for School?

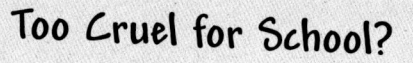

Keeping himself to himself, Lavender didn't make many friends or even many frenemies at Super School, despite being president of pretty much all the super-intelligent know-it-all clubs. He spent a lot of his time telling his teachers what to do. Even at six years old, he knew so much more than any of them about pretty much everything.

Lavender's Super Class

Simon Growl, eat your hairs out!

TNSGCC
THE NATIONAL SUPER GLOOPER CHOIR CHAMPIONSHIP

Class titles: Honour-role student and Head Boy

Voted most likely to: Succeed in everything he does.

Voted least likely to: Be scared of the dark (side).

Most likely to say (under his breath): "Mwaaah, haa, hah!"

After school he was a regular, and much valued, soloist soprano in the school choir. Apparently he was infamously known and admired for his particularly terrifying and high-pitched voice.

We asked his old choir master his thoughts on Lavender and he said: "He was already showing signs of what a true child mon-star he was, at such a young age!"

Go, Lavender!

MOSHI GENIUS FLIES THROUGH SCHOOL IN JUST TWO YEARS !

Most likely to become:
Infamous

Specialist subjects:
Roxology, Smasher-matics, Moshlingology, Fizzycs, Sm'art, Doof Ball, Musick, Katsuma Wrestling and pretty much every other subject you can take at Super School.

Extra-Curricular achievements:
Soprano in school choir, fastest getaway-sprint in the Cross-city running group.

President of: Geeks and Freaks Annoymous, The Moshling Chess Club (where Moshlings are used instead of chess pieces), The Genes and Geniuses Science Troupe and The Evil Cackle Choir (among others).

427894

The Super Moshiversity

Being such a goo-pendously brainy student all the way through school (he only needed two years to complete Monstro City Academy's years 1 to 13!), Lavender passed his exams with flying colours. Waving goodbye to his school days, he chose to study Superness and Moshlingology at the Super Moshiversity, and left home to stay in its grimy, slimy halls of residence. His parents were a little disappointed, as they wanted him to pursue a career in the family business, but they were far too scared of their little one to even think about suggesting it.

On his very first day at Moshiversity, Lavender met a fellow student named Elder Furi. (Who was known as Younger Furi at the time, purely because he was a lot younger than he is now.)

With their super intellects and immense scientific knowledge, the two geniuses hit it off like a test tube on fire!

BANG!

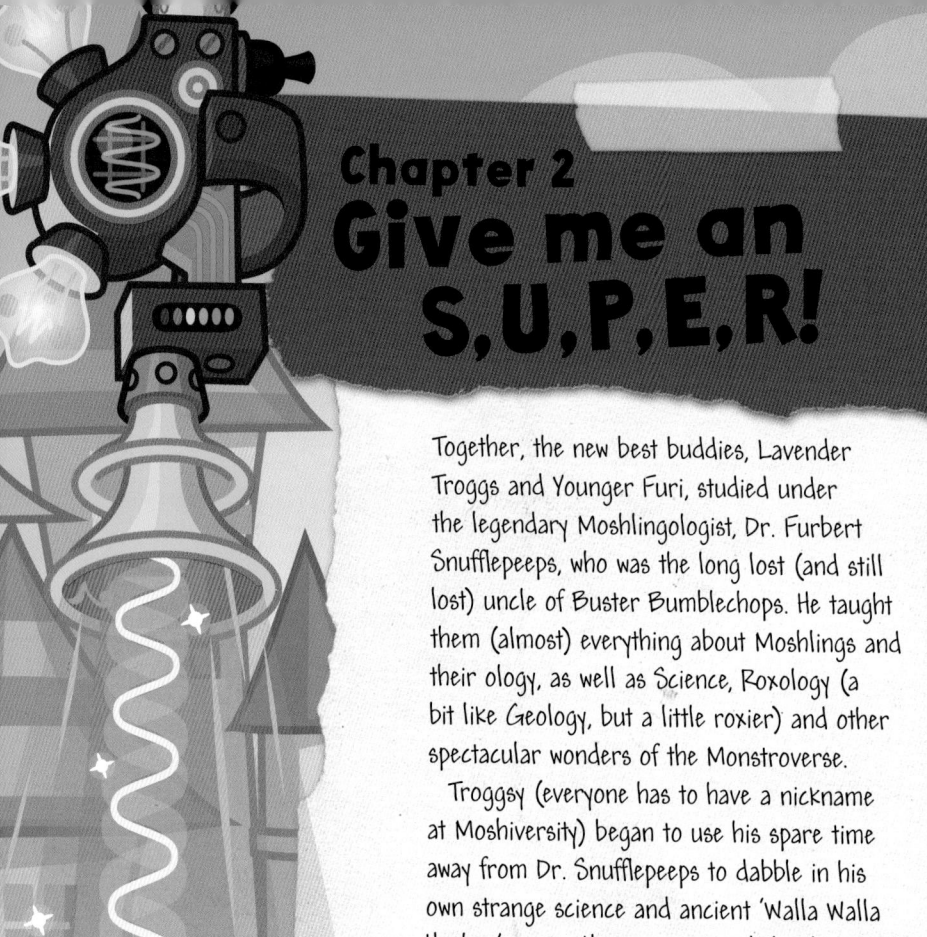

Chapter 2
Give me an S,U,P,E,R!

Together, the new best buddies, Lavender Troggs and Younger Furi, studied under the legendary Moshlingologist, Dr. Furbert Snufflepeeps, who was the long lost (and still lost) uncle of Buster Bumblechops. He taught them (almost) everything about Moshlings and their ology, as well as Science, Roxology (a bit like Geology, but a little roxier) and other spectacular wonders of the Monstroverse.

Troggsy (everyone has to have a nickname at Moshiversity) began to use his spare time away from Dr. Snufflepeeps to dabble in his own strange science and ancient 'Walla Walla Hoohaa' magic. He was convinced that he could find a way of harnessing the power of Rox in order to make himself Super, without all the annoying studying, exercise and hard work of having to go to Super Moshiversity.

"There has to be a fast solution to becoming super!" he would chant over and over to himself. "Surely, I haven't wasted two years of my life at school for nothing?" He most certainly wasn't about to waste time at Moshiversity, when he could be doing bigger and better things on his own.

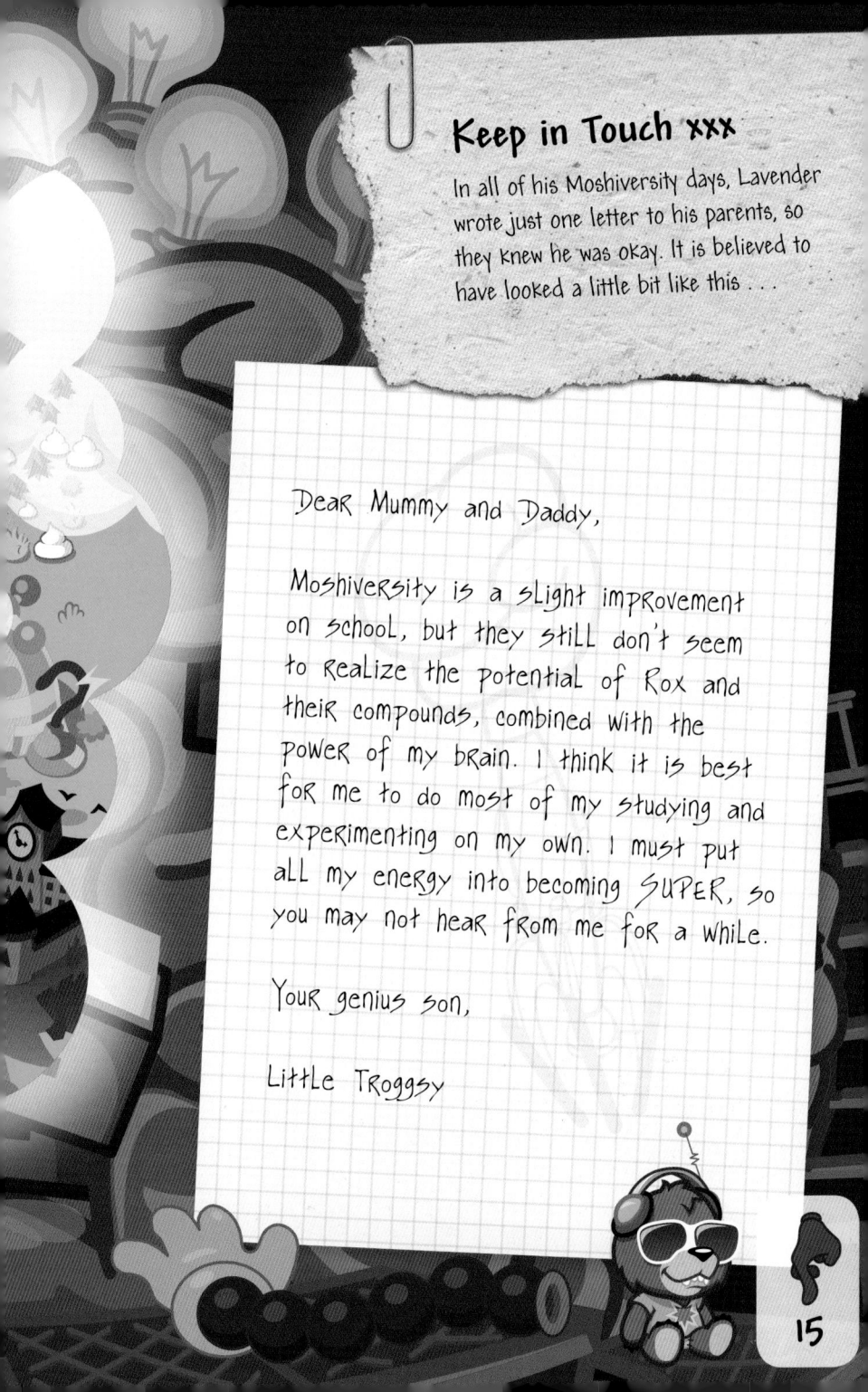

Keep in Touch xxx

In all of his Moshiversity days, Lavender wrote just one letter to his parents, so they knew he was okay. It is believed to have looked a little bit like this . . .

Dear Mummy and Daddy,

Moshiversity is a slight improvement on school, but they still don't seem to realize the potential of Rox and their compounds, combined with the power of my brain. I think it is best for me to do most of my studying and experimenting on my own. I must put all my energy into becoming SUPER, so you may not hear from me for a while.

Your genius son,

Little Troggsy

In reply, Strangeglove's parents sent him the following scare package.

To Little Troggs, our dearest darling son,

To us you will always be super! Please find enclosed a little s'care package to help you out in your darker and slightly less super days.

- A Packet of Freeze-fried Mutant Sprouts for those long nights studying and experimenting in the lab.
- 'How to Take Over the World in 3 Simple Steps' (We know you already realize how to do this, but this book sure does make for some entertaining bedtime reading.)
- A few Rox. These are not for your experiments, but to buy yourself something nice with.
- Some Real Human Ear Wax to polish your shiny gold buttons. We know it may be heading towards the Glunge Age and everyone's wearing black, but we still think it's important for you to be our little shining star. After all, gold is your favourite colour.

We hope you are taking good care of yourself and making lots of new friends at Moshiveristy.

All our love,

Mummy and Daddy

xx

Troggsy ripped open his parents' scare package and this is what really happened to the contents:

•The book was torn up and used to heat the bubbling bottles in the lab.

•Lavender tried (but failed) to harness the power of the Rox to make himself a delicious super supper.

•The Mutant Sprouts were fed to his Lab Bats.

•The Ear Wax was melted down and used to fix a broken conical flask.

17

It Takes Two

It was around this time at Moshiversity that Lavender joined forces with a mysterious partner. Little did he know that this would turn his life completely upside down, forever! This unnamed individual, whose identity still remains hidden to this day, funded Lavender's experiments, so he no longer had to use earwax to fix things. He even set him up in a brand new high-tech laboratory deep beneath Main Street, in the glamorous ancient sewerage system of Monstro City. The lab probably looked a lot like this . . .

This shadowy secret backer slowly began to have a very bad influence on Lavender, persuading him to speed up his research by experimenting on poor little Moshlings. Sniff, sniff!

HOW I WILL BECOME SUPER!!

INITIAL EXPERIMENTS

Day 1

Day 2

Day 3

Day 4

Lavender loved sketching Moshlings and new ways to experiment on the little critters in his notebooks. With all his new equipment, he soon became a Moshling expert extraodinaire, a great draftsman and even a superb engineer.

$$\diamond + \quad = \enspace ?$$

$$(E=mc^2) + \quad = \enspace \text{MONSTRO}^2 \enspace \text{CITY}$$

So, Lavender began to experiment on Moshlings, over and over again. He was determined not to stop until super powers were within his grasp . . .

21

Chapter 3
Nothing's Gonna Stop Me!

Lavender may have had great ideas for his 'how to become super' experiments on paper, but he was struggling to actually make them work. Trying to operate his crackpot creations and carry out his complicated theories on his own, was proving *très difficile*. (That's French for 'very difficult', don't you know!)

Lavender realized that he needed a co-scientist, someone who had a similar sized brain and intellect to himself, someone who had the potential to become super, someone who knew that *très difficile* meant 'very difficult', and most importantly, someone who meant business in the world of super science . . .

"Hmm," he sighed, thinking to himself. "Unfortunately, that rules out pretty much everyone I know, except for my pal, Younger Furi. I suppose it is inevitable that it is he who must be my partner."

When Lavender explained what he was doing and asked for his help, Younger Furi was (unsurprisingly) shocked.

Lavender refused to tell him who his mysterious backer was. Younger Furi felt like he had no other choice but to inform the authorities at the Super Moshiversity about what was going on.

After this, Lavender was thrown out of the Super Moshiversity! Luckily, being his usual over-achieving genius self, he'd already passed several exams without even lifting a paw, so they had no choice but to let him graduate.

Fortunately, we can prove this, as this photo sits in Lavender's mummy and daddy's house.

Unfortunately, the day this picture was taken marked the last time they ever saw him properly. Now, they just get the occasional slippery sighting of him around town like the rest of us.

Furious at being thrown out of Moshiversity, mainly because of all the free equipment he could get his paws on there, but determined to continue his research, Lavender disappeared to his secret lab. And that is where he stayed, all day and all night.

His anger at the way that he had been treated, and at Younger Furi going behind his back, made him work harder and harder at his experiments. He threw everything he had into his work, (quite literally – he even used his underpants to make a catapult!).

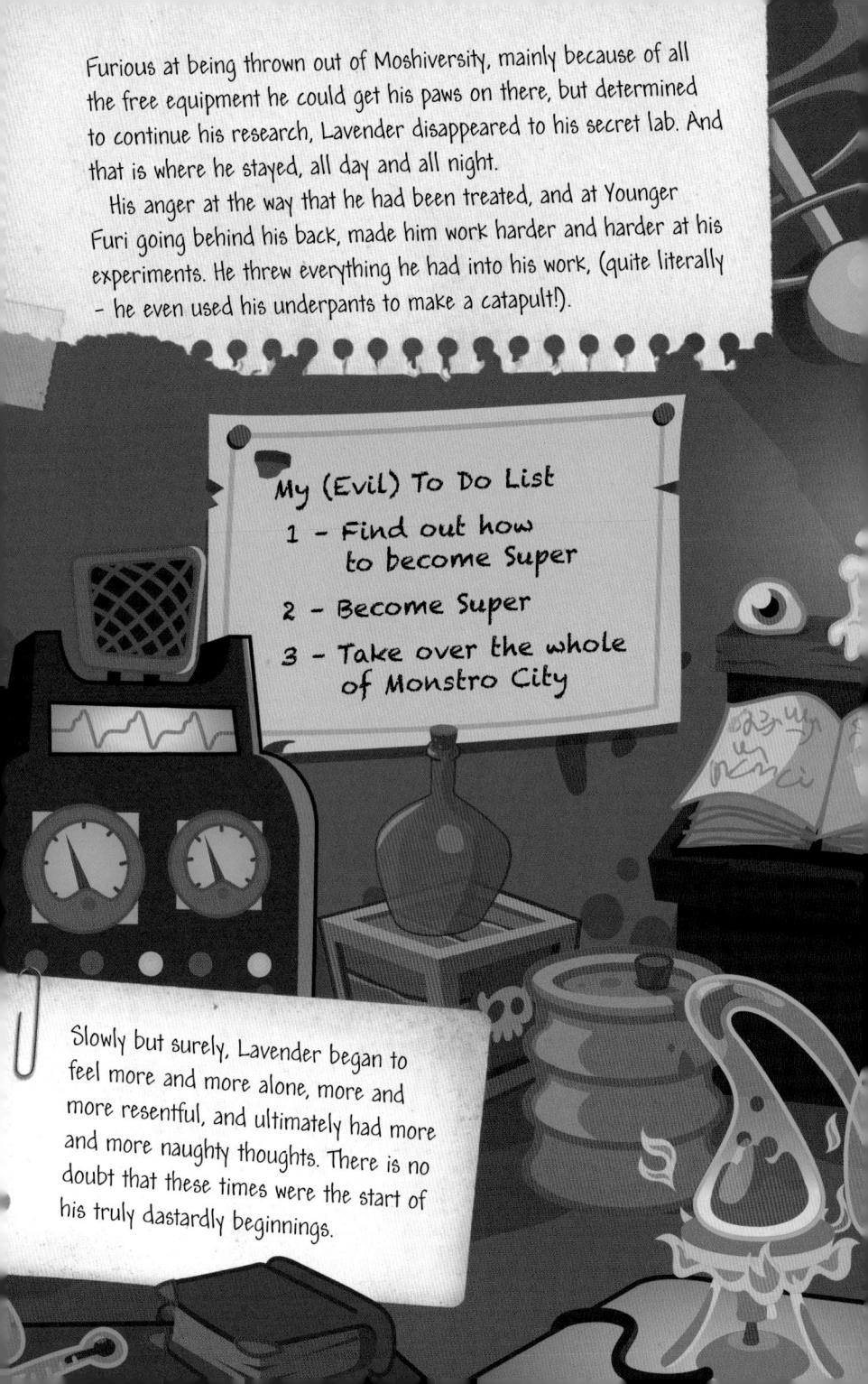

My (Evil) To Do List
1 – Find out how
        to become Super
2 – Become Super
3 – Take over the whole
        of Monstro City

Slowly but surely, Lavender began to feel more and more alone, more and more resentful, and ultimately had more and more naughty thoughts. There is no doubt that these times were the start of his truly dastardly beginnings.

Lavender became obsessed with becoming super, barely ever slept and became a super workaholic. He did nothing else, but work, work, work and he saw no one. Harking back to his choir days, and not content just whistling while he worked, he tried writing music and motivational chants to curb his loneliness and keep him working. To this day, it is said that you can sometimes hear him chanting to himself in the distance as he heads off on another getaway . . .

First Monstro City, then the WORLD!

One very late night, whilst
snacking on a string of his
favourite Silly Sausages and
singing and working at the same
time (never a good idea), a
deranged Musky Husky (whose
brain had been jumbled up by a
prototype 'Noodle Bamboozler')
came up to Lavender in his lab.
The Husky mistook Lavender's
hand for a pile of sausages and
chewed it like a shoe . . .

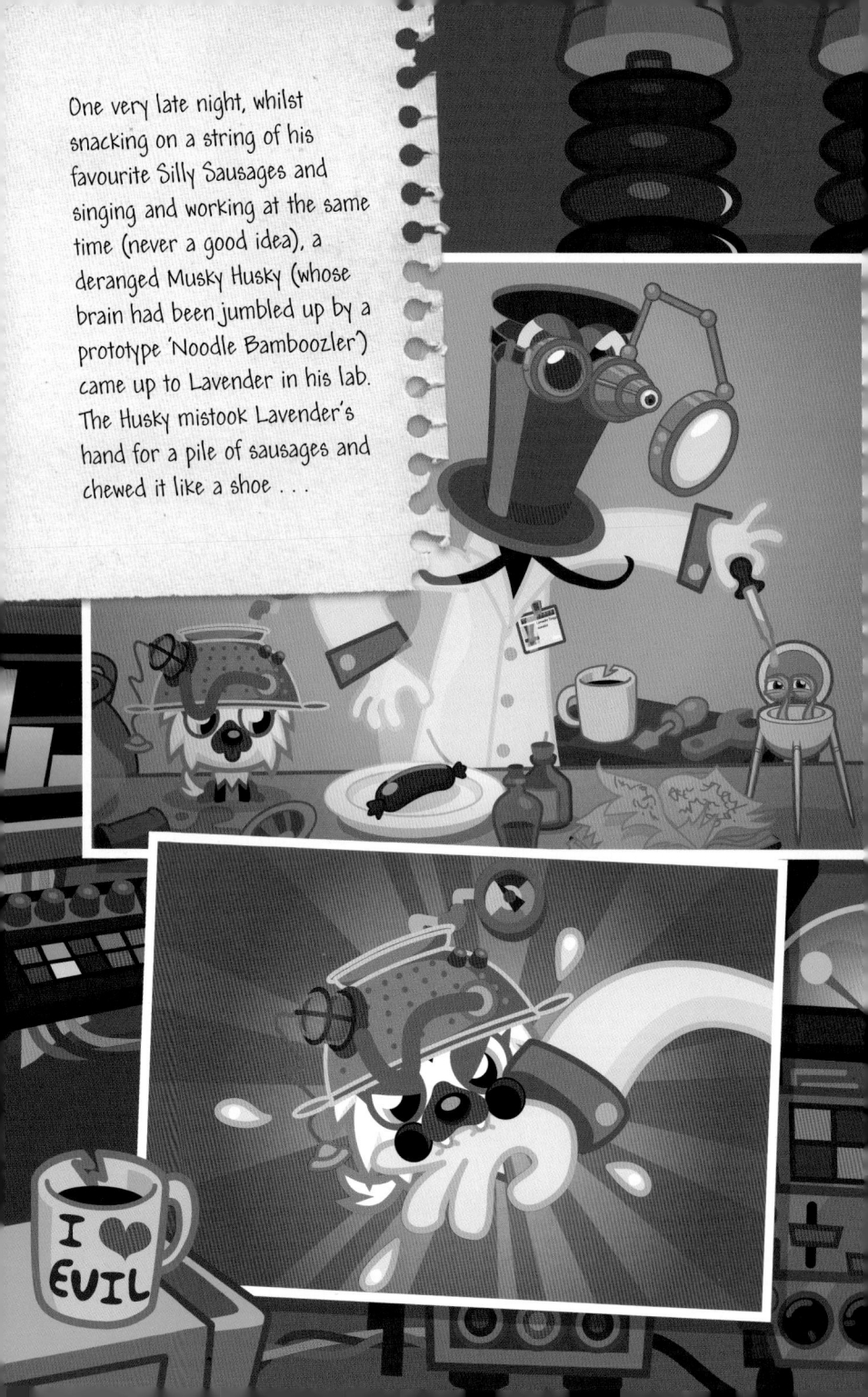

What happened next is a riddle wrapped in a Moshi mystery inside an enigma! No Moshi really knows exactly what went on because Lavender simply vanished into thin air! Locals only realized something was afoot (or should that be 'ahand'?) when they heard an ear-splitting yell from below the ground and saw the mangled remains of Lavender's gloved hand sticking out of a dumpster on Main Street.

"Eww! Yuck!" the residents who saw it gasped in disgust.

Chapter 4
Doctor, Doctor, Lend me a Hand!

Lavender survived of course, but he was left with a little bit of a dilemma. He needed a helping hand (quite literally!) to come to his rescue. Luckily, his mysterious boss was already on the case and sent him a mail order catalogue for criminals and evil masterminds who had been in similar situations before. Apparently it was pretty common to lose a body part whilst engaged in dastardly deeds and experiments, so there were plenty of goodies to choose from!

Have you lost a body part in a brawl?

IS YOUR WARDROBE MISSING THE PERFECT OUTFIT TO SCARE EVERYONE AROUND YOU?

Or are you simply looking for the perfect disguise for a cover-up operation? Whatever your dastardly dilemma - do not fear. Evil Genius Gear is here! You too could be Monstro City's Next Super (Evil) Model, as this criminal collection will cater to all of your wicked needs!

Gauntlets

Can crush solid rock!
One size fits all.

* These come with complimentary can of lubricating slime.

Oven Gloves

You don't need to be on Monster Chef to need these, they're also perfect for incendiary experiments of an evil nature.

Boxing Gloves

Pack a punch with these! Knockout selection of colours to choose from.

Wolf Mitts

Never suffer from itchiness again!

Hook

No evil mastermind would be complete without a good old fashioned hook. Amazingly versatile in the right hands . . .

Fingerless

We even provide a free finger removing service to go with them.

Driving

When you're driving your BaddieLac, the last thing you want is a loose grip on the wheel. Get these!

Evil Sock Puppet

The perfect companion to wear on your hand. Very obedient. Will perform simple tasks with limited instruction.

Rubber

Caustic chemicals won't penetrate these. Great for making mega weapons.

Clown

Make your victims smile.

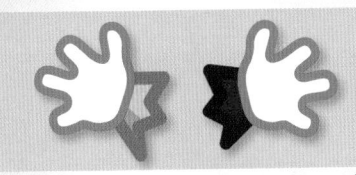

Crystal Ball

Stop living in the past. Don't bother about the present. Start looking into the future.

Wing it!

Want something a bit more uplifting? Try some wings instead!

Angel Wings
Heavenly!
Should you
wish to repent!

Fairy Wings
Latest see -
through technology.

Bling Wings
No explanation
needed!

Stripey

Stripes are back in.

Flowery Mitts

Flowers are a sign of peace and tranquility. So probably not great for evil masterminds.

Claws

Snap up a bargain with these.
Chop chop! What are you waiting for?

Robot Claw

The genius is in its simplicity. It simply grabs you straight away.

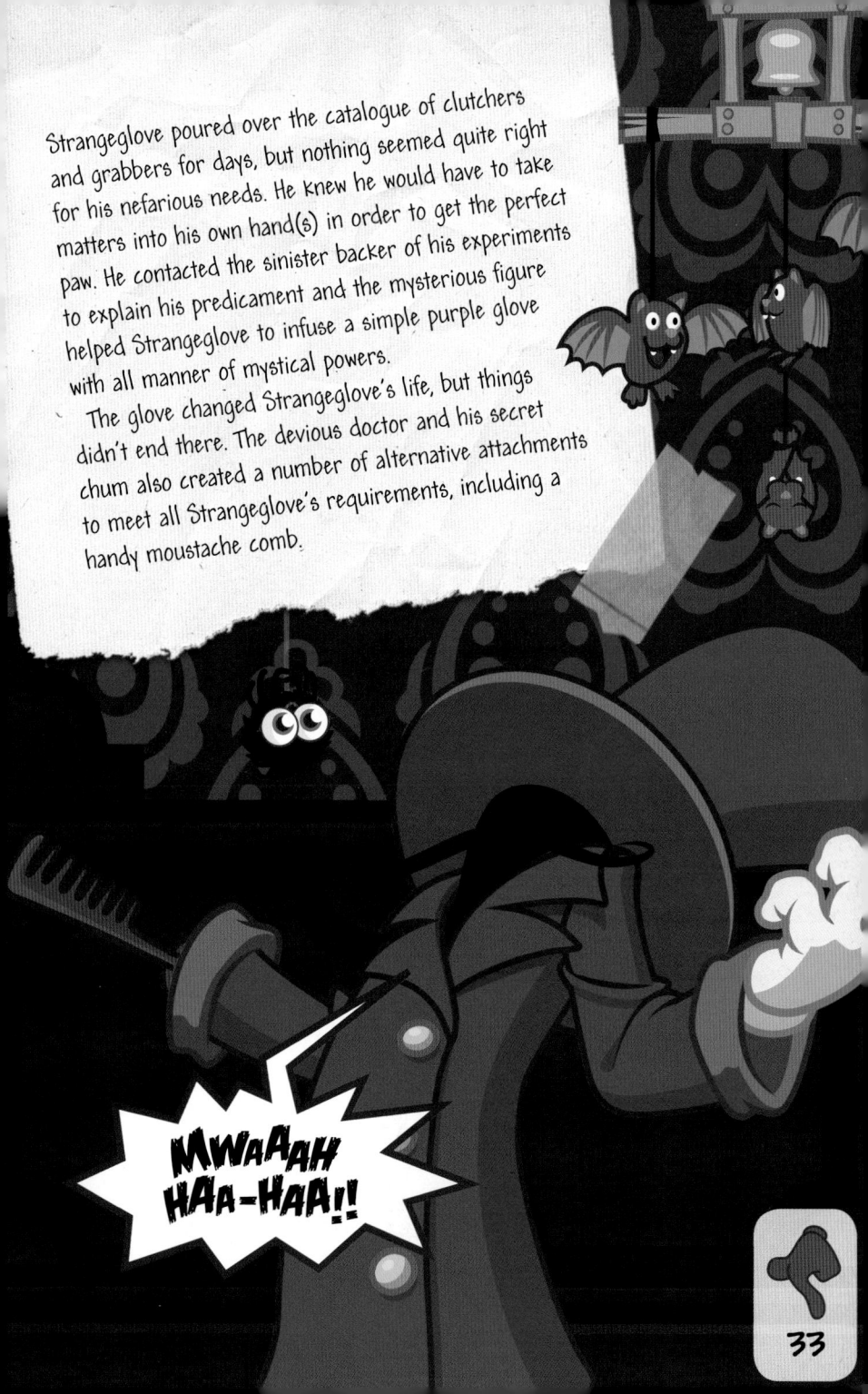

Strangeglove poured over the catalogue of clutchers and grabbers for days, but nothing seemed quite right for his nefarious needs. He knew he would have to take matters into his own hand(s) in order to get the perfect paw. He contacted the sinister backer of his experiments to explain his predicament and the mysterious figure helped Strangeglove to infuse a simple purple glove with all manner of mystical powers.

The glove changed Strangeglove's life, but things didn't end there. The devious doctor and his secret chum also created a number of alternative attachments to meet all Strangeglove's requirements, including a handy moustache comb.

MWAAAH HAA-HAA!!

The Mystically Infused Glove was a very strange glove indeed, so from that moment on Lavender, angry, twisted and deranged at his unfortunate circumstances, declared that he would now be known as Dr. Strangeglove, a cunning anagram of Lavender Troggs!

With his brand new glove in hand(!), Dr. Strangeglove continued in secret on his Rox research. His awful experience with the Musky Husky had made him even more determined to harness the power in Rox and ultimately make himself supper. Sorry, I mean super!

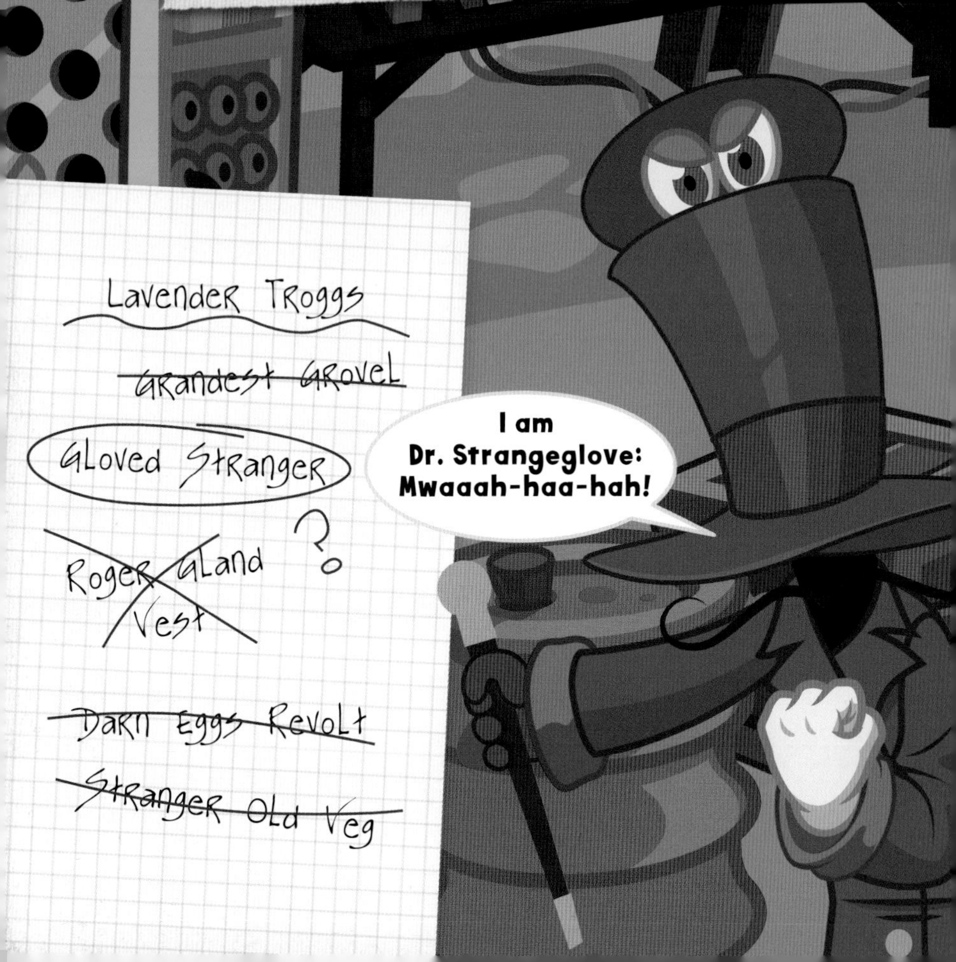

Lavender Troggs

~~Grandest Grovel~~

(Gloved Stranger)

~~Roger Gland~~ ?
~~Vest~~

~~Darn Eggs Revolt~~

~~Stranger Old Veg~~

I am
Dr. Strangeglove:
Mwaaah-haa-hah!

Unfortunately for all those cute little Moshlings out there, Strangeglove's on-going (and ill-fated) experiments led to the accidental discovery of 'Glumpodynamics'. This unexpected finding haunts the whole of Monstro City to this day.

The Glumps
Glumpitus Uglius

Through Glumpodynamics, Strangeglove realized that Moshlings could in fact be transformed into naughty little critters that would obey his every command. He called these mischievous, mindless rascals, 'Glumps', because of the noise made by his first ever Glumping Machine.

"How will Glumping help me take over the whole of Monstro City, if I'm hidden underground?" Strangeglove said to himself one day. "Besides, I need more Moshlings to turn into Glumps."

A decision had to be made. So Strangeglove decided that it was time for him to resurface and be seen again. He was determined to make a grand entrance, like all good evil criminals . . .

Chapter 5
The Glunge Age

Sinister Minister Goings On

As Monstro City came into the Glunge Age, Strangeglove decided to reappear in public for the first time after his accident. He was bored of being tucked away in complete hiding, and wanted to further his chances of being super and ruling the world. Well, ruling the city at least, for now.

Whilst underground, Strangeglove had had a series of strange dreams, some of them leading him to believe that the way to become super and rule the island, was to get into politics. The more he dreamt the dreams, the more determined he became to make them happen.

So when he surfaced, the determined and now extra naughty Strangeglove decided that he would make his grand entrance as a politician. He spent a short amount of time dabbling as a Sinister Minister for Monstro City and believed that this would help him find the power he craved.

Strangeglove's political days are a whole other story and a whole other book, involving vote-rigging and expense scandals (used to finance further Moshling experiments and a few holidays to the more exotic parts of Potion Ocean!), so we simply don't have the space to go into everything here.

I've had a dream!

Strangeglove loved the power trip of being a Sinister Minister and was often spotted campaigning around Monstro City. To get the picture of how heavy-handed (or heavy-gloved) his speeches were, take a look at this photo of him as a Minister-in-action (brought to us by Peppy's Peparazzi Political Pictures):

VOTE STRANGEGLOVE OR ELSE !!!

DONATE ROX !!

I ♥ STRANGEGLOVE

Your Moshlings NEED YOU !

I ♥ STRANGE GLOVE

Shortly after his twentieth or so political scandal, Strangeglove was (unsurprisingly) forced to resign from his position as Sinister Minister. He was once again forced to find some other way of being recognized. But he was always up for a challenge . . .

C.L.O.N.C.

Realising he couldn't keep going it alone, Strangeglove teamed up with his rich, powerful and publicity-shy boss to form a radical new gang known as C.L.O.N.C. – The Criminal League of Naughty Critters. This 'organization' was a mish-mash of felonious misfits, totally determined and utterly devoted to bringing Monstro City to its knees.

Strangeglove had slowly but surely been forgetting all that had once been good in his life; his family, Elder Furi and Dr. Furbert Snufflepeeps. He never thought back to his happy choir days, but concentrated on everything that had made him angry. He may have once been a genius, but now he was definitely an evil genius. And with such a wicked force leading it, the C.L.O.N.C. team was unstoppable!

Filename: C.L.O.N.C. 345678899

C.L.O.N.C.

Criminal League of Naughty Critters

Name: Dr. Strangeglove

Occupation: Evil deeds

Distinguishing marks: Evil purple glove, enormous hat, twirly moustache. Usually carrying a gold topped cane.

Previous convictions: Supplied on request. File too big to append to this dossier.

DS is the front face of the C.L.O.N.C. organization, relatively little is known about how high the organisation goes or where his position lies within it. All we know is he's not a nice fella and must be stopped at all costs.

C.L.O.N.C.'s Super Survival Pack of Super Goodies

Each member of C.L.O.N.C. received this Super Survival Pack of Super Goodies. (Super Baddies would be a better name for them though really.)

C.L.O.N.Card

Name: Thomas

is totally devoted to C.L.O.N.C.

C.L.O.N.C. T-shirt

C.L.O.N.C. badge

C.L.O.N.C.

C.L.O.N.C.

HOW TO SCARE ~~FOR~~ YOUR MOSHLING

I do solemnly swear to be a Naughty Critter and follow the way of our super secret dodgy leader.

C.L.O.N.C. membership form

Please sign here:

Thomas ellis

C.L.O.N.Computer

C.L.O.N.C.
needs you!

C.L.O.N.C. propaganda* began to appear all over the city, but no one had any idea what C.L.O.N.C. was, who was a part of it, or what they were planning on doing! All they could see were the initials C,L,O,N and C. Reporters at *The Daily Growl* asked the Moshi public what they thought the initials stood for. Not a lot of them made any sense!

* Please note, for those not quite as clever as Strangeglove, 'propaganda' means something along the lines of the following: exaggerated lies and made-up nonsense designed by Strangeglove in order to trick Moshlings into unwittingly becoming a part of his dastardly experiments. It seemed that the super secret organization wanted Moshis to know there was something to be afraid of, without giving away what it might be . . .

Pretty soon, through a long chain of crazy rumours and whispers, the whole of Monstro City was completely confused. "What is C.L.O.N.C.?" they would cry, day after day, night after night. Strangeglove had successfully tormented, bamboozled and frustrated everyone with mystery! His plan was working, he was beginning to become infamous throughout the city!

Chapter 6
A step too far .....

Just as C.L.O.N.C. was gathering steam, and people were beginning to get more and more scared of it, Strangeglove went missing, again!

It all started when he decided to return to Mount Sillimanjaro, which he had previously conquered as a four year-old child.

Greetings from Mount Sillimanjaro!

We don't know exactly what happened at the top of the very high mountain, but looking at these extracts from Strangeglove's expedition diary, we can conclude that somehow he must have gone one step too far in the wrong direction, after something happened with his old pal, Elder Furi. Surely Elder Furi wouldn't have pushed him, would he?*

*Please note, this is pure speculation.
Obviously Strangeglove was unable to write whilst fighting, or falling off a mountain for that matter.

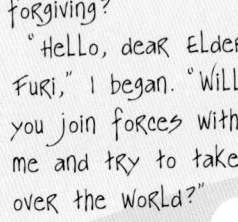

My Trip!

Day 1

I'm Super-trekking my way along the backside (mwaah, ha, ha!) of Mount Sillimanjaro. The air is very refreshing and I feel like I'm on top of the world, but realize that won't actually be true until tomorrow.

Day 2

Just bumped into me olde pal/traitor, Younger Furi at the summit. I have to say, he is now very much Elder Furi, as he's put on a few pounds and there are more than a few wrinkles on his face. I decided to forgive him for telling the Moshiversity authorities about my Moshling experiments and enlist his help once again. Who says evil doctors can't be forgiving?

"Hello, dear Elder Furi," I began. "Will you join forces with me and try to take over the world?"

¡HHHHAAAAAAAAAAAAAAAA

Ka - Pooooowwwwww!
Day 3
BLank
Day 4
BLankety bLank

So it seemed that Strangeglove's 'trip'
really was a 'trip'! We have no idea how he
survived his fall, but, just like a bad penny,
Strangeglove returned to cause trouble once again!

The Moshi public knew something was up when
there was a break-in at Buster's Ranch and lots of
poor little Moshlings started to go missing again.

"It can only mean one thing . . ." they cried.

"He's back!"

And sure enough, everyone began to see
Strangeglove loitering around the streets. They sat
on the edges of their Sausage Sofas and Toffee
Crunch Couches, awaiting his next move. Luckily,
help was at hand . . .

Two Sides to Every Story

It is a well-known fact that all scoundrels need arch rivals and someone or something trying to stop their super dark ways, otherwise the world would be a very evil place! No exception was made for Dr. Strangeglove. He had not only made Elder Furi his enemy, but a whole team of Super Moshis were on his case too!

This ancient book, which has been passed down from one Moshi generation to the next, tells us all about about the history of the Super Moshis and their mission to protect Monstro City.

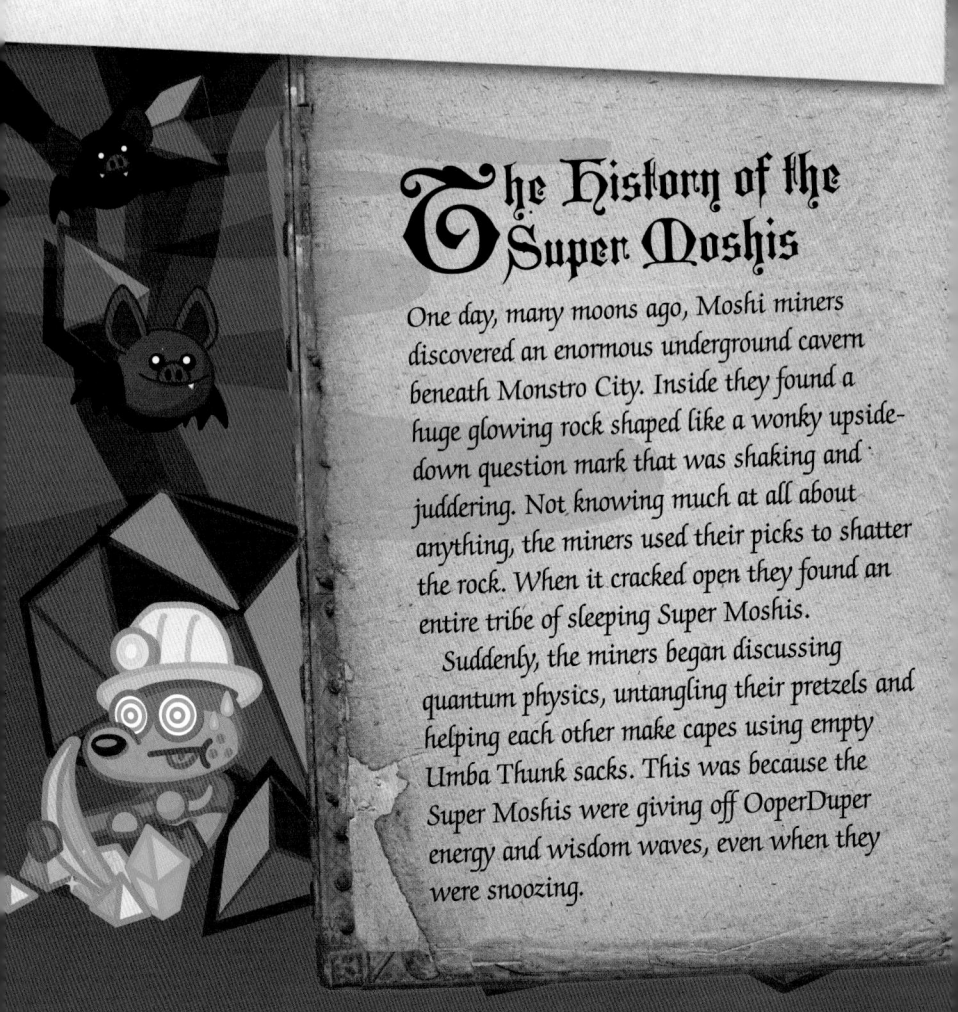

The History of the Super Moshis

One day, many moons ago, Moshi miners discovered an enormous underground cavern beneath Monstro City. Inside they found a huge glowing rock shaped like a wonky upside-down question mark that was shaking and juddering. Not knowing much at all about anything, the miners used their picks to shatter the rock. When it cracked open they found an entire tribe of sleeping Super Moshis.

Suddenly, the miners began discussing quantum physics, untangling their pretzels and helping each other make capes using empty Umba Thunk sacks. This was because the Super Moshis were giving off OoperDuper energy and wisdom waves, even when they were snoozing.

Before long, the Super Moshis stirred from their slumber, slammed their fists against their chests, pointed skywards and fell flat on their faces. (Well, so would you if you'd been asleep that long!) After a few push-ups and star jumps they got to work, dishing out nuggets of knowledge and teaching monsters how to make friends and get along.

And that's the way it stayed for many years.

Then one day, having knocked a whole heap of sense into generations of monsters, the Super Moshis suddenly disappeared. No goodbyes, no leaving parties . . . nothing. Well okay, they did stick a little note on the fridge saying 'Our work here is done' but it fell off.

And that was that, for a time . . .

Return of the Super Moshis!

But after all the mysterious C.L.O.N.C. goings-on, the Super Moshis came back! (Trumpet blast, please.) And they were determined to whup Monstro City, Dr. Strangeglove and C.L.O.N.C. into shape!

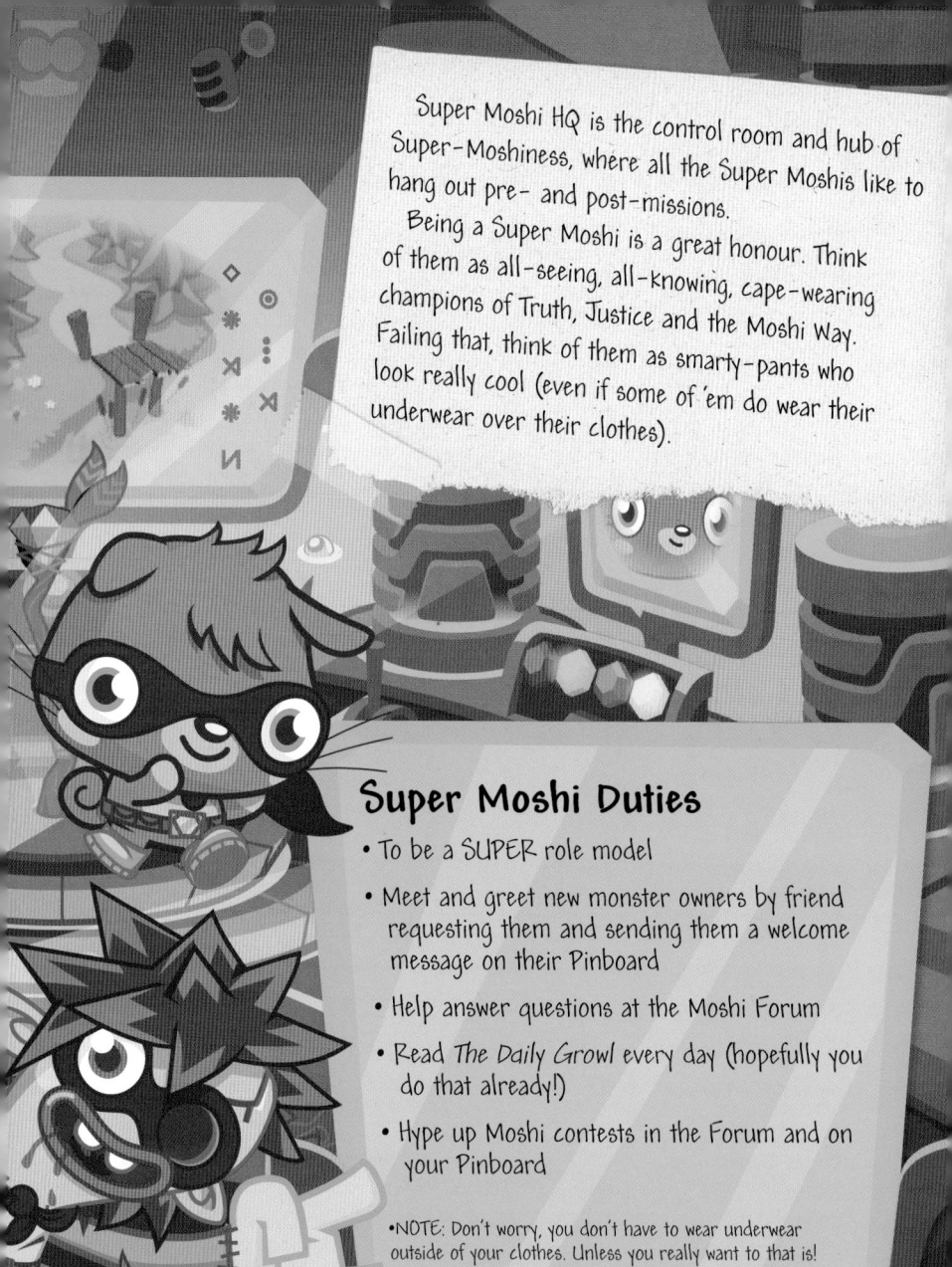

Super Moshi HQ is the control room and hub of Super-Moshiness, where all the Super Moshis like to hang out pre- and post-missions.

Being a Super Moshi is a great honour. Think of them as all-seeing, all-knowing, cape-wearing champions of Truth, Justice and the Moshi Way. Failing that, think of them as smarty-pants who look really cool (even if some of 'em do wear their underwear over their clothes).

Super Moshi Duties

- To be a SUPER role model
- Meet and greet new monster owners by friend requesting them and sending them a welcome message on their Pinboard
- Help answer questions at the Moshi Forum
- Read *The Daily Growl* every day (hopefully you do that already!)
- Hype up Moshi contests in the Forum and on your Pinboard

•NOTE: Don't worry, you don't have to wear underwear outside of your clothes. Unless you really want to that is!

Chapter 7
Present Day Doctor of Fame

So right now, in a Monstro City not all that far away from you, the battle between good and evil continues . . .

Now is a time where Strangeglove and Elder Furi, with his crack team of Super Moshis, are constantly battling against each other; a time where C.L.O.N.C. won't stop raising their ugly evil heads; a time where Moshlings keep disappearing, and then re-appearing again; and a time when things seem like they just can't get any stranger. Or can they?

Showbiz Strangeglove

In between Glumping innocent Moshlings, battling Elder Furi and the Super Moshis, and wreaking mayhem, Strangeglove has somehow also found time to go showbiz! After supposedly leaving his choir days far behind him, he has composed a fiendishly brilliant, semi-autobiographical song about his life. Assisted by that bumbling ball of badness, Fishlips, his trombone-playing Glump sidekick, Strangeglove puts on a terrifying performance.

When asked about this sideline to his usual evil-doings, Strangeglove is reported to have said, "I like having a bit of a break from those pesky Super Moshis. When I'm on stage performing, I forget about everything except for my music."

It's true – villains have all the fun!

Mwah-haa . . . mwah-hah-hah . . . muuuwaaahhahaha!

His song was a literal smash hit, with Strangeglove smashing up stages wherever and whenever he performed. There are some rumours that it may even go on to be Twistmas number one every year. And having seen his dastardly vote-rigging and scandalous ways, I'm sure the devious doctor will be able to rig the charts and make that happen one way or the other . . .

Lyrics to Dr. Strangeglove's song

Glump, Glump, Glump, Glump, Glump, Glump, Glump, Glump
The doctor will see you now . . . Mwah-ah-ah-ah-ah-aaaa!

Sneaky, sly and shifty,
Let me introduce myself:
I'm the doctor they call Strangeglove
a hazard to your health!
I'm here to wreck some mayhem
With my terrifying schemes
And Glump your silly Moshlings with my dastardly machines! MWAHAHAHA!

Chorus

Strangeglove, Strangeglove, they call him Dr. Strangeglove,
Strangeglove, Strangeglove, the one to be afraid of,
Strangeglove, Strangeglove, they call him Dr. Strangeglove,
Strangeglove, Strangeglove, Strangeglove, Strange!

I assume you think it's sinister to hold an ancient grudge
but understand it cost my hand so don't be quick to judge!
A Musky Husky mangled it and chewed it like a shoe:
he thought it was some sausages, so now this glove must do!
Don't impede my evil deeds or try to foil my plan.
Even though I wear this glove I have some helping hands!
So peak outside your window, and check behind your door.
Is Dr. Strangeglove lurking or has he called before?

Chorus

Let 'em have it Fishlips! (trombone music)
Blow harder, you spherical fool! (trombone music)
Strangeglove, Strangeglove, the one to be afraid of, Strangeglove, Strangeglove . . .
I'll show those Super Moshi's!
Oh yes, nasty!
Today Monstro City, tommorow the World!
Mu-hahahahaaaa!

Daily Growl

GLONC RULZ!

STRANGEGLOVE'S SHOWBIZ SHOWDOWN!

The Underground Disco was completely taken over last night, when Dr. Strangeglove, Fishlips (his trombone playing, lip-smacking fiend) and a group of Glump backing singers, jumped on stage. Clearing everyone else to one side, they started jamming away and knocking out their new rap tune.

Simon Growl is reported to have said, "I hate to say it, but it's actually pretty good!"

The Super Moshis may be able to stop Strangeglove from ruling the world, but there sure is no one stopping him from ruling the stage!

STRANGEGLOVE TURNS HIS GLOVE TO ACTING!

Music just wasn't enough for Strangeglove it seems. Starring with Tyra Fangs in this movie adaptation of a well known Shakesfear play, DS gave an oscare-winning performance.

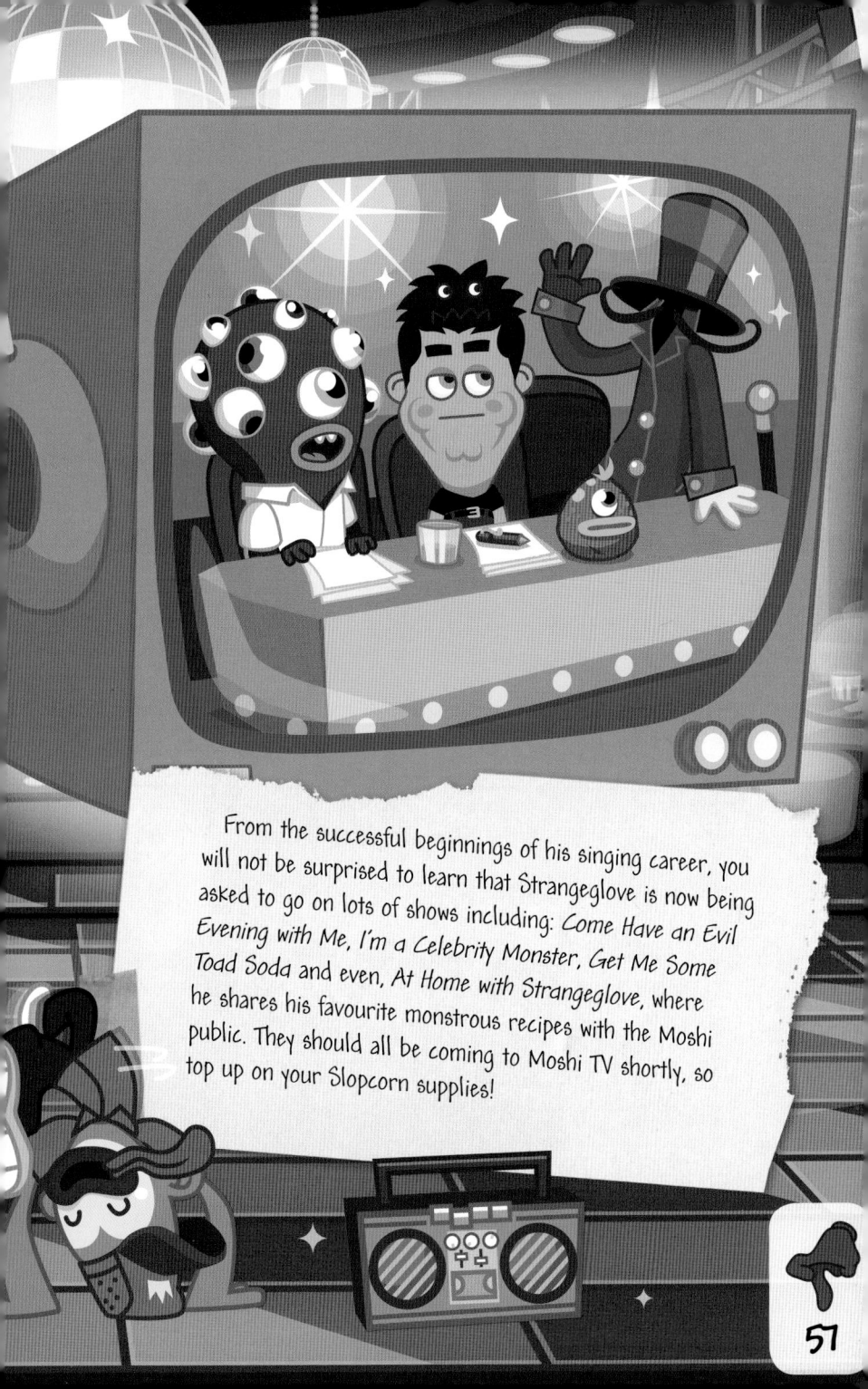

From the successful beginnings of his singing career, you will not be surprised to learn that Strangeglove is now being asked to go on lots of shows including: *Come Have an Evil Evening with Me*, *I'm a Celebrity Monster*, *Get Me Some Toad Soda* and even, *At Home with Strangeglove*, where he shares his favourite monstrous recipes with the Moshi public. They should all be coming to Moshi TV shortly, so top up on your Slopcorn supplies!

The End? - NEVha, ha, ha, ha!

"Perhaps Strangeglove's celebrity singing status is the end of all his evil-doings?!" I hear you cheer.

But no, and alas, like all truly naughty evil geniuses, Strangeglove's number one thang will always be his desire to become super and take over Monstro City . . . While on his path to celebrity fame, Strangeglove still found time to build a Super Weapon and monsternap Elder Furi. His plans were thwarted by the Super Moshis, who destroyed his latest Glumping machine and sabotaged his blueprint for the Sun Smasher 9000, saving Monstro City from certain doom! That slippery Dr. Strangeglove has fled the city and with C.L.O.N.C. still out there somewhere, he is probably plotting his next devious deeds as you read these very words!

The end (but just for now!)

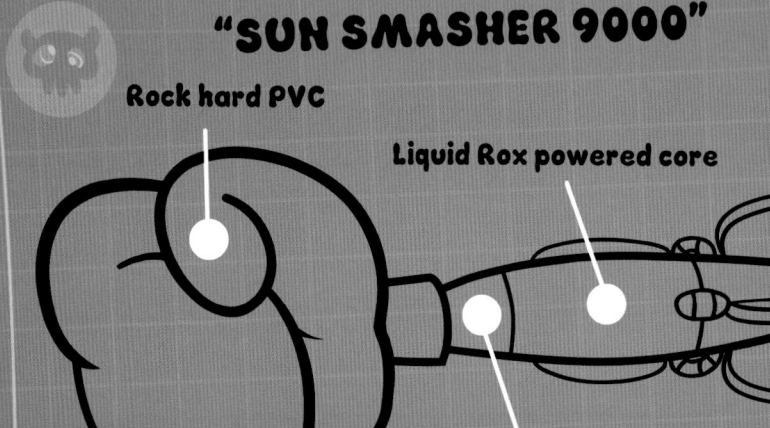

"SUN SMASHER 9000"

Turbo rocket booster

Rock hard PVC

Liquid Rox powered core

Rubber chicken

Cardboard rudder

Sun Smasher

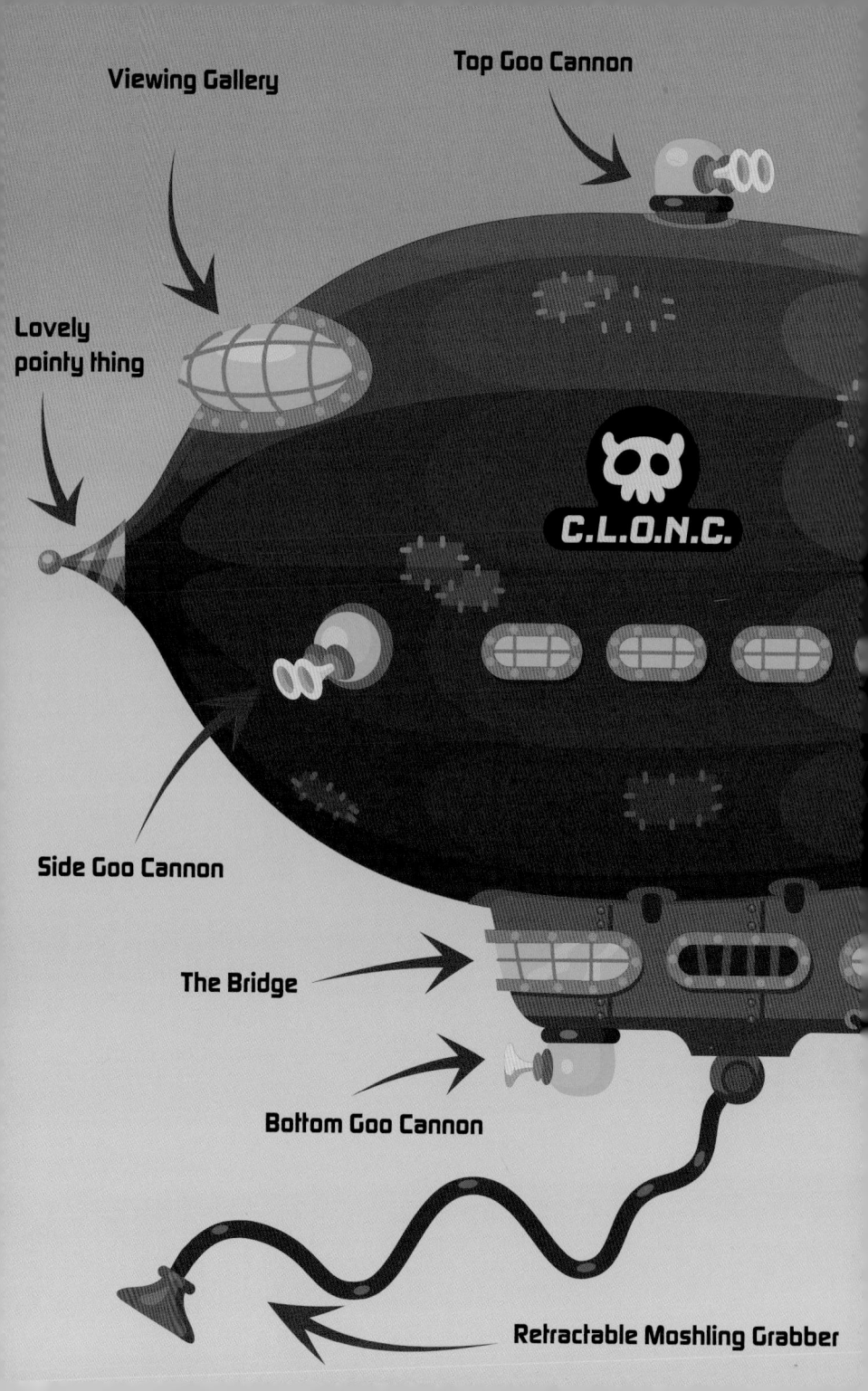

Viewing Gallery

Top Goo Cannon

Lovely pointy thing

C.L.O.N.C.

Side Goo Cannon

The Bridge

Bottom Goo Cannon

Retractable Moshling Grabber

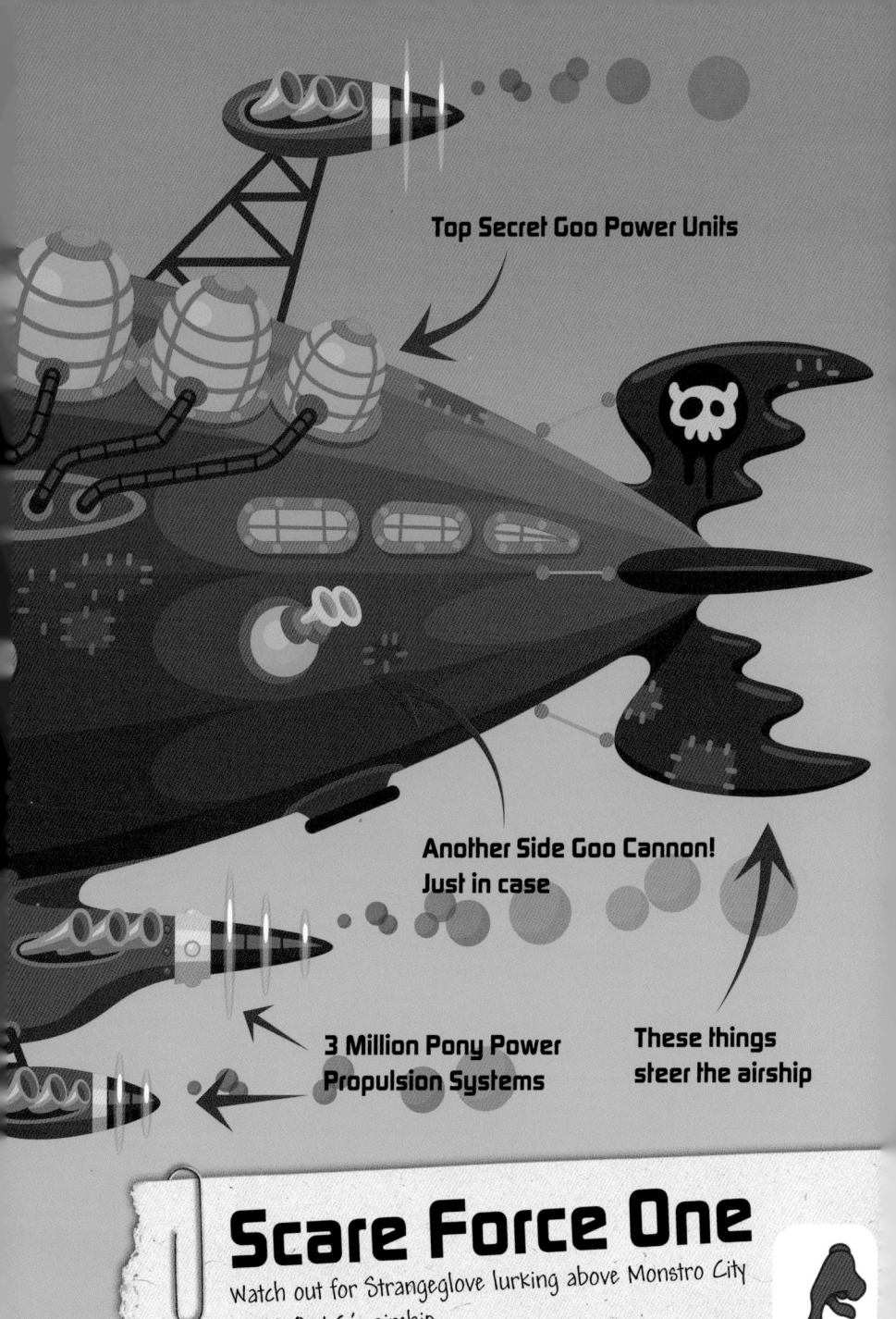

Top Secret Goo Power Units

Another Side Goo Cannon!
Just in case

3 Million Pony Power
Propulsion Systems

These things
steer the airship

Scare Force One
Watch out for Strangeglove lurking above Monstro City
in C.L.O.N.C.'s airship.

Glumpssary

Don't you just hate Glumps? Rocko does! Then again Rocko hates everything. That's why you'll often see this snaggle-toothed brute doinging along alone before attacking with a Rocko Blocko Backroll.

ROCKO

With lips like that, Fishlips should have been the lead singer in Hairosniff. Sadly this one-eyed blob of badness can't sing because those luscious lips are permanently sealed with gloop – perfect for delivering SuctionySmackeroos. Yuck!

FISHLIPS

Cheer up Bruiser, you look like you've been dragged through a hedge backwards. What's that? You have? Oh dear, it's probably because you can't help causing mayhem with your Scarface Smashes and Scowling ScrimScrams.

BRUISER

Capable of chomping up enemies in seconds with a Triple Tooth TerrorBite, this dim-witted Glump is interested in only two things: eating and perfecting that silly pink quiff. Fabio has even tried eating his teeth but they tasted glumpy.

FABIO

This greenish globbish Glump must have graduated with honours from the School of Drool because it can't stop dribbling. Not that manners matter because Freakface is a master of the Burbling Gurgling Gobstopper. Yeew, slimy!

FREAKFACE

Poo, what's that smell? Oh, it's Pirate Pong, the stinkiest Glump in town. Capable of clearing a room in seconds with a Stinky Winky Squint, this pongy pirate reeks of rotten fish and hot trash, so keep your distance.

PIRATE PONG

A Guide to Strangeglove's Glump companions.

Bloopy is feeling blue. But so would you if you had a face like a squished blueberry! Anyway, don't take pity because this badly-behaved blob loves splatting Moshlings with Mega Glump Thumps. Ouch!

BLOOPY

Quick, run! Podge is boinging along Main Street – and that means you might get caught in a Lumpy Lasso! It's true because Podge has a super long icky-sticky tongue – ideal for rounding up poor little Moshlings!

PODGE

Is that facial fuzz for real or is it just a terrible disguise? Who knows because Mustachio is too busy barking orders and attacking Moshlings with scritchy-scratchy Bristly Brush Offs to answer silly questions.

MUSTACHIO

Say hello to the Glump that looks like a complete nerd – but keep it quiet because behind those daft goggles Ned is a total fiend, especially when mangling Moshlings with Goggle-Plop Grapples.

NED

What's got three eyes, buck teeth and stupid hair? Squiff, of course! This naughty nugget might be golden but when it comes to being friendly Squiff is worthless, especially when letting rip with a Squiffy Stinkbomb! Urgh!

SQUIFF

Mad, bad and dangerous to know, Black Jack is one mean Glump. Even other Glumps steer clear of this fearsome ball of fury – especially if he's knocking down the citizens of Monstro City with a Cannonball Cavalcade!

BLACK JACK